D0232200

THE STORY OF A SNAIL WHO DISCOVERED

THE IMPORTANCE OF BEING SLOW

ALMA BOOKS LTD
3 Castle Yard
Richmond
Surrey TW10 6TF
United Kingdom
www.almajunior.com

The Story of a Snail Who Discovered the Importance of Being Slow
first published in Italy by Ugo Guanda Editore in 2013
This edition first published by Alma Books Ltd in 2017

© Luis Sepúlveda, 2013
by arrangement with Literarische Agentur Mertin Inh. Nicole Witt
e.K., Frankfurt am Main, Germany

Translation © Nick Caistor, 2017

Cover and inside illustrations © Satoshi Kitamura, 2017

Printed in Great Britain by CPI Group (UK) Ltd, Croydon CR0 4YY

ISBN: 978-1-84688-413-9

All rights reserved. No part of this publication may be reproduced, stored
in or introduced into a retrieval system, or transmitted, in any form or
by any means (electronic, mechanical, photocopying, recording or otherwise), without the prior written permission of the publisher. This book is
sold subject to the condition that it shall not be resold, lent, hired out or
otherwise circulated without the express prior consent of the publisher.

The Story of a Snail Who Discovered the Importance of Being Slow

Luis Sepúlveda

Translated by
Nick Caistor

Illustrations by
Satoshi Kitamura

ALMA BOOKS

ABOUT THIS STORY

A few years ago in our garden, my grandson Daniel was closely observing a snail. All at once he looked up at me and asked a very difficult question: why are snails so slow?

I told him I didn't have an answer there and then, but promised I would give him one some day.

Since I pride myself on keeping my promises, this story is an attempt to respond to his question.

And, naturally, it is dedicated to my grandsons Daniel and Gabriel, to my granddaughters Camila, Aurora and Valentina, and to all the slow snails in my garden.

The Story of a Snail who Discovered the Importance of Being Slow

ONE

In a meadow close to your house or mine, there lived a colony of snails. They were quite sure they lived in the best place in the whole wide world. None of them had travelled as far as the borders of the meadow, let alone to the tarmacked road that began where the last blades of grass grew. As they had not travelled, they had no way of making any comparisons. They did not know for example that, for squirrels, the best place to live was at the very top of beech trees. Or that for bees there was nowhere nicer than the wooden hives at the far end of the meadow. The snails could not compare these things, and they didn't care. They thought that the meadow where the rain helped lots and lots of dandelion plants to grow was the very best place to be.

When the first days of spring arrived and the sun began its warm caress, they woke from their winter sleep. Making a huge effort, they raised their shells enough to stick their heads out, then stretched out their tentacles with eyes on the tips. They were so happy to see that the meadow was covered with grass, tiny wild flowers and, above all, delicious dandelions.

Some of the older snails called the meadow Dandelion Land. They also called home the leafy calycanthus bush that each spring grew with renewed strength from leaves scorched by the winter frosts. The snails spent most of their time underneath its leaves, hidden from the birds' greedy gaze.

Among themselves they simply called one another "snail". This sometimes caused

confusion, which they resolved with slow determination. For example, it might be that one of
them wanted to talk to another one. It would
whisper: "Snail, I want to tell you something."
At this, all the others would turn their heads.
Those to the right would move them to the left;
those to the left to the right; those in front would
look behind; those behind would stretch their
tentacles; all asking: "Is it me you want to tell
something to?"

Whenever this happened, the snail that wanted to talk to another one would crawl slowly, first left and then right, forwards and then backwards, repeating all the time: "I'm sorry, it's not you I want to tell something to." On and on until they finally reached the snail they did want to talk to, generally about something related to life in the meadow.

They all knew they were slow and silent. Oh-so-slow and silent. They also knew that this slowness and silence made them vulnerable. Much more vulnerable than other animals who could move quickly and raise the alarm. So as not to be frightened by this slowness and silence, they preferred not to mention it. Slowly and silently, they accepted what they were.

"The squirrel squawks and leaps from branch to branch. The goldfinch and the magpie fly quickly. One of them sings, the other caws. The cat and the dog can run quickly too. One meows, the other barks. But we are slow and silent.

That's life: there's nothing we can do about it," the oldest snails would whisper.

But among the group there was one snail who, despite accepting an oh-so-slow life of whispers, still wanted to know the reason why they were slow.

TWO

Like all the others, the snail who wanted to know why they were oh-so-slow had no name. This worried him a lot. He thought it was unfair, and whenever one of the older snails asked him why he wanted a name, he replied, also in a whisper: "Because the calycanthus is called that – calycanthus – which means that for example when it rains we say we're going to shelter beneath the calycanthus leaves. And the delicious dandelion is called dandelion. This means that when we say we're going to eat some dandelion leaves, we don't get it wrong and end up eating nettles."

But the arguments of the snail who wanted to know why they were so slow didn't really interest the other snails. They muttered to one another that things were fine as they were. It was enough to know the names of the calycanthus, the dandelion, the squirrel and the magpie, as well as the meadow that they called Dandelion Land. They felt they needed nothing more to be happy as they were: slow, silent snails, busy keeping their bodies wet and putting on enough weight to survive the long winter.

One day, the snail that wanted to know why they were oh-so-slow heard the older snails whispering. They were talking about the owl who lived in the trunk of the oldest and tallest of the three beech trees that grew on the edge of the meadow. They said he knew lots of things, and that on nights when the moon was full he hooted a long list of trees called walnut, chestnut, elm and oak, which the snails had never heard of and couldn't even imagine.

So the snail decided to ask the owl why they were so slow, and slowly, oh-so-slowly, he crawled to the oldest beech tree. When the dew was making the meadow glisten with reflections of the morning sun, he left the shelter of the calycanthus leaves. He arrived at the tree when the shadows were spreading over the meadow like a silent blanket.

"Owl, there's a question I want to ask you," he whispered, raising his body up towards the bird.

"Who are you? Where are you?" the owl wanted to know.

"I'm a snail and I'm at the foot of your trunk," he replied.

"You'd better climb up to my branch. Your voice is as weak as the growing grass. Come on up," the owl invited him. So the snail began another oh-so-slow journey.

As he climbed to the treetop, his way lit only by the distant gleam of the stars twinkling through the leaves, the snail passed a squirrel sleeping curled up with her babies. Higher up, he crawled round the web a hard-working spider had woven between the branches. By the time he reached the owl's branch, the snail was tired out, and the light of a new day had renewed all the beech's shades and colours.

"Here I am," whispered the snail.

"I know," replied the owl.

"Don't you need to open your eyes to see me?"

"I open them at night and see all there is to see. During the day I close them, and see all there was to see. What is your question?" asked the owl.

"I want to know why I'm oh-so-slow," whispered the snail.

At this, the owl opened his huge round eyes and studied the snail closely. Then he closed them again.

CHAPTER TWO

"You're slow because you're carrying such a heavy weight," he said.

This answer didn't convince the snail. He had never found his shell heavy. Carrying it around never tired him, and he had never heard any other snail complain about the weight. He said so to the owl, and waited for the bird to finish swivelling his head around.

"I can fly, but I choose not to. Before, a long time before you snails came to live in the meadow, there were many more trees than you see now. There were beeches and chestnuts, elms, walnut trees and oaks. All of them were my home. I used to fly from branch to branch. Now the memory of those trees weighs on me so heavily I prefer not to fly. You're a young snail, and everything you've seen, everything you've experienced, the sweet and the sour, the rain and the sun, the cold and the night – all that travels with you. It weighs you down, and since you're so small, the weight makes you slow."

"And what's the use of me being oh-so-slow?" whispered the snail.

"I don't have the answer to that. You'll have to find it yourself," said the owl. He fell silent, and the snail knew he wouldn't listen to any more questions.

THREE

After talking to the owl, the snail who wanted to know why they were so slow returned slowly, oh-so-slowly, to the calycanthus bush. He found the others taking part in what they called "the tradition".

Once, although none of them could remember exactly when, the wind blew some coloured, regularly shaped leaves into the meadow. Their edges were smoother than any the snails had seen among the trees and plants they knew. These leaves glided and danced in the air, until they finally landed on the wet grass. On the leaves were strange black signs, and human

beings who were so still and small they did not look as dangerous as they usually did to the creatures of the meadow. This amazed all of them.

Slowly, oh-so-slowly, they crawled over the fallen leaves. They studied these unmoving human beings lining up in front of a surface that was filled with what must have been very delicious foods, because at the tip of these leaves the snails could see them smiling as they carried away their meals.

"Someone, I don't remember who, told me that humans devote their lives to repeating things, movements and ways they called 'traditions'," said one old snail.

"This tradition of eating together doesn't seem such a bad idea," commented another snail. The others waved their little tentacles to show they agreed: they thought this tradition of eating in a group was a wonderful idea.

From that day on, the colony of snails abandoned their habit of eating alone at all hours of the day, as and when they were hungry. Instead, they decided to all eat together at sunset, gathered beneath the thick calycanthus leaves. To make the tradition more pleasant, they took turns to be the ones who whispered questions and those who whispered replies.

"What is there to eat?" one would ask.

"Dandelion. Delicious dandelion leaves," another would answer.

"I'd like to eat something delicious," one would say.

"I can recommend dandelion," another would reply.

Thanks to this "tradition", every evening beneath the calycanthus bush the snails got together to eat small dandelion leaves and to whisper about the tireless way the ants worked, about how stand-offish the locusts were as they leapt across the meadow without saying hello to any of them, and about the dangers lying in wait for snails. They were frightened by caterpillars, who were able to pull them off the calycanthus leaves however hard they clung on, and by beetles, whose powerful jaws were capable of smashing their shells. But what the snails feared most were human beings. When one snail went "crunch", then another, and another, they all became afraid. They knew that because of the clumsy way that humans moved, planting their big, heavy feet anywhere, many of them would not survive to enjoy the pleasant sunset tradition.

The snail who wanted to know the reason why they were oh-so-slow used to take part every evening in the tradition of eating and whispering about all that had happened that day beneath the calycanthus bush. He also kept on asking why they were so slow, and why none of them had names.

"Well, let's see," replied one of the oldest snails, who was tired of so many questions. "We're slow because we don't want to go leaping about like locusts or to fly like butterflies. As for having a name, you ought to know that only humans are able to name the things and creatures in the meadow. And that's enough silly questions, or we'll drive you out."

This threat really upset the snail who wanted to know why they were oh-so-slow and wanted to have a name. He was also upset because none of the other snails supported or defended him. And even more upset that some of them were whispering: "Yes, yes, he has to go. We want to live in peace."

Stretching his neck as far as he could, he swivelled his eyes to look at each and every one of them. Then, raising his voice as loud as his tiny mouth permitted, he said:

"Very well then, I'll go. And I'll only return when I know why we're oh-so-slow, and when I have a name."

FOUR

Still eating, the other snails watched as the snail who wanted to know why they were oh-so-slow and wanted to have a name crawled away slowly, oh-so-slowly, and vanished among the tallest blades of grass in the meadow.

When sunset gave way to darkness and the shining stars were reflected in the blades of grass and plants wet from the dew, the snail decided to look for a safe place to spend the night – a smooth surface where he could fix his body and curl up inside his shell. Slowly, oh-so-slowly, he went first to one side, but all he found was more grass. He set off in another direction, until his tiny eyes spotted a low stone he thought would make a splendid shelter. He climbed slowly, oh-so-slowly, up it, until he came to a flat spot on the top. He stretched out his muscles to cover an area as wide as the opening of his shell, then pulled them in. Swaying from side to side, he made sure he was stuck fast, and settled down to sleep.

It was completely dark inside the shell. His neck, head and tentacles with the little eyes at the tip were a solid lump that fitted in snugly, and yet he couldn't fall asleep.

He kept thinking that perhaps he had made a mistake by leaving the group and the safety of the calycanthus bush. At the same time, a voice that wasn't his whispered that there must be a reason for snails to be so slow, and that having a name that was his own and no one else's, a name that made him unique and unmistakable, must be wonderful.

Just as he was thinking all this, the stone moved. He could hardly feel it, but it did move. He'd heard terrible stories from older snails about an animal called a hedgehog, which had a body all covered in spikes and could upturn even heavy stones when it was searching for food.

The stone moved again. The snail heard a weary, oh-so-weary voice that said:

"Who... has... climbed... up... on... me?"

He had also heard from the older snails that the wind whistling through reeds could sound terrifying, but the voice below him didn't frighten him.

"Are you a talking stone?" he asked.

"A stone... that talks?... If that's... how you... see me... I don't mind... but... who... are you?..."

"I'm a snail, and I've stuck myself to you in order to spend the night here. Is that all right?"

"A snail... yes... you can stay... snail... you... and I... are alike..."

After saying this, the stone moved again until it could settle on the grass. The snail wondered why he had said they were alike.

"Why do you talk so slowly? Are you a slow being, like me?"

"I… talk… slowly… because… I have… oh-so-much time… Sleep… well… snail…"

The snail asked her more questions, but got no reply. The sound of steady breathing reached the smooth surface where he had fixed himself. It was the contented sound of a creature sleeping beneath the sheltering stars. He too fell asleep happily.

The snail woke when he sensed once more that the stone or slow creature was on the move. Slowly, oh-so-slowly, he relaxed his muscles and poked out his head. Extending his little tentacles, he saw he was on a beautiful surface. It was almost as beautiful as the blanket of moss the stones covered themselves with in the dampest part of the meadow.

"You… decide… snail… either you climb off… or… I'll take you…" said the weary voice.

Slowly, oh-so-slowly, the snail slid down until his body touched the grass. To his surprise, he found he had not spent the night clinging to a talking stone, but to a creature who had a hard shell like him. Beneath it, he could see four very sturdy legs, a wrinkled neck, a mouth that wasn't scary and a pair of half-open eyes peering at him.

"I... am... a tortoise..." he said when he saw the snail stretching his neck to look at him.

The snail had never seen an animal this big that did not frighten him. When he told him so, the tortoise brought his head closer so that he could hear him. Then he told him that in time he would grow much bigger still. In his slow, careful way of speaking, as though the effort to find the exact words tired him out, he told the snail that he too had once been a small, scared creature. But he was related to the huge turtles that lived so long that they needed immense bodies to store the memory of all they had seen, heard, feared and loved – as well as the memory of anger, joy, the reasons for heat and cold, for terrifying fire and refreshing water.

The tortoise began to move. Even though she moved slowly, oh-so-slowly, with every step she took, the snail had to make a huge effort to stay level. After only a short while, he felt worn out and asked the tortoise if he could climb back onto her shell.

"I can't keep up with you – you go too fast for me," he said.

"Me… fast? That's… the first… time… I've ever… heard… that… yes… snail… climb… aboard…" replied the tortoise.

When the snail had climbed on and settled down behind the tortoise's head, he asked her where she was going. The tortoise replied that this was the wrong question – that he should have asked where she was coming from. With that, she strode out, and the snail felt as if the grass in the meadow was flying by at a speed he

had never seen. The tortoise explained that she herself came from the forgetfulness of human beings.

"I don't know what it means to forget, and I don't know human beings either," whispered the snail.

The tortoise slowed down. She told him of how happy she had been to find a house where there were always fresh lettuce leaves, the juicy flesh of tomatoes and the sweet taste of strawberries. Some young humans had looked after her and spoilt her. They even made her a bed of straw at one end of their garden. Then, when cold rain shortened the days, and later when snow turned the yard into an unfriendly, frozen surface, these human beings took her into the house and let her sleep in a lovely warm corner.

"It sounds as if you had a good time," said the snail.

"I … can't… complain… but… humans… grow up… and forget…" the tortoise sighed. She told him how, as time passed and the young humans grew into adults, they paid her less and less attention. They hardly fed her, and finally decided she was getting under their feet, and so left her out in the meadow.

This story made the snail feel sad. He was even sadder when the tortoise, searching among the many words she knew, told him she went back and forth across the meadow, meeting some creatures who were friendly and others who were not. She would forever be far from the place she had called home, heading for an unknown destination that had the cruellest name. It was called exile.

"Can I go with you?" whispered the snail.

"First… tell me… what… you… are… look-ing for…" replied the tortoise. So the snail told her he wanted to know why snails were oh-so-slow. He also wanted to know his own name, because the water that falls from the sky is called rain, the fruit from the spiky bushes are called blackberries and the smell from hives is called honey. He also told her that this wish of his had made the other snails angry. They had even threatened to drive him out of the meadow. So he had decided to leave on his own, and not to return until he had an answer and a name.

The tortoise searched even more carefully than usual for the words to answer him with. She told him that she had learnt many things while she had been with the human beings. She said that whenever a human asked awkward questions like: "Do we have to go so fast?" or "Do we really need to own so much to be happy?" they would call him a rebel.

"Rebel? I like that name," whispered the snail. "Did the humans give you one?"

"Yes… because… I never… forgot… the way… out… and… the way… back… they… called me… Memory… but… they… forgot… me."

"So, Memory, shall we go on together?"

"All right… Rebel…" the tortoise replied. She turned her body round slowly, oh-so-slowly, and explained they would go back the way she had come, because she wanted to show the snail something important. Something that would help him understand that they had been heading in the same direction even before they had met.

FIVE

The sun was in the middle of the sky by the time they reached the edge of the meadow the oldest snails called the "End of Life". It was a dark, level surface that spread out as though a slice of the night sky had become stuck to the ground and was covering all the grass and wild flowers.

On the far side of this dark strip they could see human beings. Some of them were busy placing what to the snail seemed like stones one on top of the other. Astonished, he whispered that the humans were as hard-working as bees when they were building a hive. The tortoise, searching for the words in the well of her memory, explained that these humans were building houses. Still more human beings and their young would live in them. They would arrive with all their possessions in huge, bustling animals with big round feet, animals driven by metal hearts.

"Perhaps they've fixed a boundary. On that side of the dark strip there will be human beings, and on this, the creatures of the meadow," said the snail.

"It's… not that… simple… Rebel… look… at the… sides…"

Perched on top of the tortoiseshell, the snail extended his neck and the little tentacles. What he saw at the two ends of the black strip made him shiver. He could not find any words to describe it. The tortoise could sense the snail's dismay. With her usual calm, she explained that the dark ribbon was called a street or road, that the huge animals alongside the humans were called machines, and that the thick dark cloud they were spitting out was known as tarmac. Human beings did not like to use their feet to get around, because they thought that was too slow. Instead, they preferred to use metal animals, which they admired and envied more the faster they went. What the snail could see were the humans at work covering the meadow with tarmac so that their powerful animals could rest there.

"I don't know exactly what I feel, but I don't like it," whispered the snail.

"It's… called… fear… Rebel… fear…"

"Then don't call me Rebel. I thought that name would make me feel brave, very brave."

The tortoise turned slowly, oh-so-slowly, round, and marched back into the meadow. As she went along with the snail on her back, she explained there was no reason to be frightened of fear.

Searching through her memory, she told him that human beings often said that a true Rebel felt fear, but conquered it.

When the stars advised them to stop their march and get some rest, the two friends had something to eat before they went to sleep. The tortoise gently chewed some small flowers; the snail had some delicious dandelion leaves.

"What... will... you... do... Rebel?"

"I don't know. I don't know whether to find out why I'm oh-so-slow, or to go back to my friends and warn them of the dark danger looming over the meadow."

Chewing on the last flower petals, the tortoise told him that if he wasn't an oh-so-slow snail but could fly as swiftly as the kite or leap like the locust, or was as agile as a wasp – coming and flying off again in the blink of an eye – perhaps there would never have been this meeting between two such slow creatures as a snail and a tortoise.

"Do… you… understand… Rebel…?" the tortoise ended, her eyes closed.

"I think so. My slowness allowed me to meet you. And you gave me a name, and showed me the danger. Now I know I have to warn my friends."

"Your… determination… is… what… makes… you… a Rebel…"

Ready for sleep, the snail began to climb onto the tortoise's shell, but she told him she preferred them to sleep side by side. The snail waited for the tortoise to fold in her four legs and for her rough neck and head to disappear in her shell, then he stretched his muscles, stuck himself to the grass and made himself comfortable inside his own shell.

He had a disturbing dream. He saw the thick black cloud that the humans' machines spat out spread all over the meadow. It covered the calycanthus bush, and his friends were swallowed up by the darkness.

He was woken by the sun's caress warming the thin wall of his shell. Slowly, oh-so-slowly, he put out his neck, stretched it, and then his tentacles with eyes on their tips. When he opened them, he saw the tortoise was no longer there. A trail of flattened grass stems showed the path the tortoise had taken: the opposite direction to the calycanthus.

"Thank you, I'll always keep you with me, Memory," the snail whispered. Then oh-so-slowly he began the return journey to meet his friends.

SIX

On his way back to the calycanthus, the snail came across some ants. They were carrying tiny drops of honey in an orderly line. Obeying the laws all the meadow creatures respected, the snail came to a halt. Otherwise, if he crossed the path they were making without warning them, his wet trail would make them lose their way.

"Ants, I need to cross your path to warn my friends of a great danger," he said, arching his head until it almost touched the ground.

"And what might this great danger be, if you please? Keep in line there!" said an ant that looked slightly older than the rest. He wasn't carrying anything, but kept a strict eye on the other ants who were.

So the snail told them about the human beings, and how they had started to cover one end of the meadow with a thick layer of something that was blacker than a starless night.

"That sounds very serious, but I can't decide what you must do. My job is to lead these carriers to the anthill. I said 'stay in line'! Come with me and talk to our queen."

The snail set off with the ant, but could not keep up with the frantic rhythm of its feet. He crawled on oh-so-slowly, and by the time he reached the anthill, the queen was waiting for him, surrounded by her court.

"You took your time. You shouldn't keep a queen waiting," the older ant scolded him, but the queen ordered him to be quiet and approached the snail.

"Is what you say true? Is it true that the humans are covering the meadow in a blanket blacker than the depths of the earth?"

"Unfortunately for all the meadow creatures, it is true. A tortoise called Memory took me to the edge and I saw…"

"It's not the first time this has happened to us. We have to be on our way!" the queen ordered. At once, the ants began to swarm out of the anthill, carrying tiny bit of leaves, drops of honey and seeds – all the food they had kept stored underground.

"We have to thank your slowness, snail. If you were as quick as a rabbit, or could slither as swiftly as a snake, you wouldn't have seen and warned us. Do you have a name?"

"I'm called Rebel. That's the name Memory gave me."

"Memory, Rebel – thank you both," the queen said. She shouted out: "Time to leave!" and joined the long line of ants streaming from the anthill.

Before the sun caressed the meadow with its dying rays, the snail had also warned the beetles of the danger. After hearing his news, they also thanked him for his slowness. If he had been as quick as a lizard or a grasshopper, he wouldn't have seen or warned them.

The snail watched as the beetles hurried out of their den. They went off pushing little balls of food in front of them.

Rebel, the snail who now had a name and was starting to learn the reasons for being oh-so-slow, was exhausted by now. He decided to rest before going to meet his friends, who would at that moment be following their tradition of eating together beneath the caly-canthus leaves, unaware of the danger. Before he could fold his body inside his shell, he realized that many of the night-time creatures of the meadow were stirring: the earthworms, who feared the sun, were crawling along, leaving their wet trail along the grass; the fleeting glow-worms swooped to light the way for the caterpillars; and the tiny green frogs croaked as they leapt in search of a puddle.

Rebel began to feel drowsy. Just as he was about to fall asleep, he heard a tiny voice calling out from beneath the grass.

"Are you the snail I've heard so much about?" said the voice.

"Yes, and who might you be?"

Right next to him, the ground bulged upwards. The grass gave way to a small mound of earth, and a creature with a pointy nose poked out its head.

"I'm a mole. There are creatures who live flying high over the meadow – there are others who live among the grass – and others who live below ground. Is it true that the humans are going to cover it all with a layer of black ice?"

The snail answered that yes, unfortunately it was true. After thanking him, the mole disappeared back inside his mound. He wanted to warn his friends that they had a lot of digging to do.

Rebel, the snail who had a name and was learning more and more reasons why he was oh-so-slow, settled down once again. But so many questions had slipped inside his shell with him, he couldn't sleep.

What if his friends didn't believe him? What if his companions beneath the calycanthus bush thought he was just awkward and odd, as they had when he had wanted to have a name and know the reason why he was oh-so-slow? And if they did believe him and accepted the need to lose their home, the Dandelion Land, where would they go?

SEVEN

Beneath the calycanthus leaves, the snails who were unaware of the coming danger barely turned their heads to look at the returning snail.

"You don't seem to have gone very far," whispered one old snail.

"Are you here to eat or ask more questions?" sniggered another one, still chewing on dandelion leaves.

"If I remember rightly, you said you'd be back when you had a name and knew the reasons why we were oh-so-slow. So what do you have to tell us?" another snail added slyly.

Ignoring their scornful looks, Rebel approached oh-so-slowly until he reached the welcome shade of the calycanthus leaves. Then he told them about his meeting with the tortoise called Memory.

"Oh! What an interesting encounter! A slow meadow creature bumps into an equally slow creature. And what did you do? Have a race?" another of the old snails mocked him.

Once again, Rebel ignored the hurtful remark. He told them about everything he had seen, and how the humans were invading the meadow and covering it with a choking black blanket that could only bring sorrow.

This time his words caught the attention of the youngest snails, who became worried. But the older ones saw this as a challenge to their authority.

"None of us has ever seen any of these things you talk about. Besides, it's well known that tortoises have a habit of inventing things that don't exist," said one.

"And even if it were true," said another of the oldest snails, "who's to say the humans intend to come as far as the calycanthus?"

"We'll never leave our place beneath the calycanthus. We'll never leave Dandelion Land," said another of the old snails.

So then Rebel told them about the other creatures in the meadow. He told them that the ants, the beetles, the earthworms and the moles were all leaving, and that he thought they should do the same.

"This is intolerable. You're a rebel. I demand you show us what you're talking about. Otherwise keep quiet and leave, and don't come back," warned the oldest snail of all.

Rebel thought that his friends were so slow they would never be in time to see how the other meadow creatures were leaving, carrying or pushing their food with them. But his eyes fell on the long stems of the calycanthus, their tight purple flowers reaching up to the sky.

"Climb up here with me," he whispered.

Slowly, oh-so-slowly, Rebel started to climb one of the stems that was swaying in the wind. A few young snails followed him. And, in order not to lose their authority, so did a few of the older ones.

They took the endless amount of time that slow creatures take before they reached the tips of the stems. It wasn't easy for them to stick their bodies to the petals at the top, but once they had done so and trained their eyes on the far end of the meadow, what they saw filled them with dread.

Remembering what Memory had told him, Rebel explained that the strange shapes next to the humans were called machines. The dense smoke preventing them seeing beyond the border was grass burning beneath the black covering. At first this was thick and soft like fresh mud, but soon it became as hard and impenetrable as stone.

"They're very close," whispered the oldest of the snails. Fear had made him less sure of himself.

"We must get away!" said the youngest snails. Then slowly, oh-so-slowly, they began to climb back down.

Once they were safely beneath the calycanthus leaves, they all looked with new respect at the snail who had brought them the warning.

"You were right. You've learnt a lot on your journey, and you'll have to be our guide when we leave. Before you went, you said you wouldn't return until you had a name. Did you find one?" asked the oldest snail.

"It is what you called me before we climbed the stems. My name is Rebel. That's what Memory named me."

"Where shall we go?" asked one of the young snails.

"We'll leave Dandelion Land, but we can find another one. Let's head for a new Dandelion Land," said Rebel.

And so, slowly, oh-so-slowly, with all the pain of saying goodbye to their lost Home, the snails began to leave the calycanthus bush.

EIGHT

Slowly, oh-so-slowly, the band of snails made their way through the grass. They were sad, and felt that this sadness slipped inside their shells, making them heavy. None of them dared voice their fears. They kept turning their heads back towards their beloved calycanthus, until after a long while they could no longer see it. Then one of them noticed they were heading for the end of the meadow – that is, towards the humans.

"Just a moment. What kind of a leader are you? You're leading us straight into danger," he whispered, terrifying the rest of the snails even further.

Rebel came to a halt. He reminded them that the birds and squirrels who lived in the most ancient beeches used to settle in their branches to watch the sun go down. And the rabbits and frogs in the meadow did the same.

"Many creatures give silent thanks for the warmth they have received. Even flowers close slowly to keep in the last bit of heat. But as beings of the shade, we never stop to watch as the sun gives way to darkness," said Rebel.

'That's right. We avoid the sun because we need the wetness of our bodies to live. But I still don't understand why you're taking us to where there are humans," said one of the oldest snails.

"Because during my journey with Memory I studied the humans closely. I saw that they don't put the black blanket on the far side of the wood-and-stone shells they call their houses. Perhaps humans also like watching the sun drop down to its nest of fire."

"Perhaps! Perhaps! That means you're taking us to somewhere we've never seen but we might perhaps reach, although there's no certainty," another of the old snails snorted.

"And I say perhaps we shouldn't leave the caly-canthus – that perhaps the humans won't reach there – that perhaps we should abandon this senseless adventure," said another of the oldest snails in the group.

"Yes, let's go back to the land we should never have left!" cried several more snails. So the group split into two. Nearly all the older snails began to return oh-so-slowly to the calycanthus plant. The younger ones swivelled their eyes to peer at Rebel.

"It's true I cannot be certain of finding the new Dandelion Land. It's true I don't know where it is, or how long it will take. It's true I don't know if we'll meet great dangers, or if all of us will get there. But I know this new Dandelion Land is in front of us, not behind. I'm going on. You can come with me or go back."

Slowly, oh-so-slowly, Rebel moved forward. When he turned his head, he saw all the snails were following him. This didn't make him feel proud or happy. At that moment he thought he would have preferred them not to follow him, so that he would only be responsible for his own fate. The snails put their trust in him, and that made him afraid. But then he remembered Memory telling him that a true rebel felt fear but conquered it. So he carried on crawling slowly, oh-so-slowly, across the grass.

NINE

By the time the snails reached the hard, black strip the humans called a road, the first shadows were blurring the outlines of the grass and flowers.

"I'm scared. Nothing grows on this black blanket," one of the snails whispered.

"What shall we do now?" asked another one.

"Wait for the humans to rest. Memory taught me that just as we curl up inside our shells, so human beings do the same in their houses. They stretch out their bodies and rest," Rebel replied.

The human beings' houses had holes in them that lit up as if glow-worms were inside.

The snails were hungry and so tasted some of the blades of grass growing at the roadside. They soon stopped: the leaves had a strange, unpleasant taste that was like the smell coming from the black surface in front of them.

Inviting in the night's silence, the stars were shining as the holes in the houses fell dark one by one. Rebel knew they would have to find the new Dandelion Land quickly, because the darkness of the nights was growing longer and longer. The air was growing colder, and they needed to feed a lot for their long sleep, safe from frost and snow.

"Now," whispered Rebel. For the first time, his body came into contact with the stiff black layer covering everything that until recently had been a fertile meadow.

The surface seemed hard and rough, and the stench coming from it irritated his sense of smell. But it was smooth, and there were no obstacles to climb or avoid. Although they moved slowly, oh-so-slowly, this meant they could move easily across it.

"I can feel a very pleasant heat," whispered one snail, coming to a halt.

"It's true. There's a warmth rising into my body," said another one, who also stopped.

"This heat is very nice. Why don't we stop and carry on when the sun comes up again?" asked a third snail. Rebel remembered Memory had told him that, because it was black, this surface didn't reflect the rays of the sun and kept in the heat. And this was a trap, Memory had explained. Some meadow creatures, like hedgehogs, gave in to the warmth of that dry ground. They became drowsy, and so were easy prey for the enormous animals that human beings moved around in.

"No. We have to go on. We mustn't stop. We have to do all we can to reach the far side," Rebel managed to say before a loud roar paralysed them.

From one end of the road, a being with enormous shining eyes came roaring towards them, bathing them in a blinding light. It sped past like a stormy wind. Once it had gone, the snails saw that several of them were no longer there.

Trembling with panic like all his friends, Rebel ordered them to go on without stopping, before this or any other terrifying animal came past again.

It was a painful march. All they could whisper was their fear or how much they regretted having followed him. When they finally reached the far side of the road, they found shelter in a cold, circular cave where a trickle of water ran. They stuck their bodies to the sides of the cave and fell asleep, overwhelmed by pain and tiredness.

All the snails were asleep, apart from Rebel. He stayed on watch at the entrance to the cave. The eyes on the tips of his tentacles peered into the dark night.

He soon began to feel very tired as well. He was about to spread his body inside his shell when the noise of something stirring the air startled him.

"Snail, don't be afraid," said the bird.

Rebel emerged slowly, oh-so-slowly, from the cave. He recognized the owl who lived in the meadow's most ancient beech.

"You're flying. Doesn't all you've seen weigh you down any more?"

"It weighs me down even more than before, but I have to fly," replied the owl. Tucking his head under a wing to hide his sorrow, he told the snail that none of the three beeches was there any more, and that the humans and their machines were faster than all the beings in the meadow.

"What about the calycanthus?" Rebel dared to ask.

"It's not there either. Very little of the meadow we knew is left," the owl sadly replied.

"I think we'll stay in this cave," whispered Rebel. "At least we're safe here."

"It's not a cave, and you're not safe there," said the owl. He explained they were in something the humans used. It was a kind of long, thick worm connected to a metal mouth which, when they gave an order, let out a powerful stream of water.

"I've failed. I'll never lead my friends to the new Dandelion Land. If only I knew as much as you – but I'm just an oh-so-slow snail," Rebel moaned.

"It's in my nature to observe and know. And don't complain that you are slow, snail. It was thanks to a tortoise who every few steps turned her head to see if she was being followed that I learnt about a young snail called Rebel – a brave snail who, despite the danger, was courageous enough to warn his companions and is now trying to save them. Don't give up, Rebel. I'll help you get out of here."

The darkness was beginning to fade when, obeying the owl's orders, the snails stuck their bodies to a piece of wood. They watched as the bird spread its wings, took several quick steps, beat the air and took off high into the sky.

The owl glided round in circles, its huge wings outstretched, until it found a breeze that brought it swooping back down to the piece of wood. Picking it up in its powerful claws, it flew up again, its wings beating fast because the wood with the snails on was very heavy.

From high in the air, the snails saw the sun rise. When they risked poking their tentacles out of their shells, they saw that nearly all the meadow had disappeared beneath the black blanket.

The owl flew on for what to the snails seemed a very long time. The ground, the trees, the silver ribbons of streams and the houses where the humans lived flashed by at an unbelievable speed for the slow meadow creatures. Then the owl swooped down and laid down its load very close to some big trees.

"This is a chestnut wood. The humans will take a long time to destroy it. Go on, and leave behind the trunks with moss growing on them. You'll come to a clearing. That's where there is grass and wild flowers, but make sure to get there as quickly as you can, because the trees are already losing their leaves. The cold and the snow will soon take over the landscape. I can't carry you to the clearing, because I wouldn't be able to take to the air again."

The snails thanked the owl for his help. They watched as he flew away and disappeared above the treetops.

"Let's go on," whispered Rebel. He was the first to head for the fresh green patch clinging to the trunk of a chestnut tree.

TEN

Slowly, oh-so-slowly, the snails entered the wood. They crawled over the ground carpeted with leaves: some were the colour of honey, others were darker; some were complete, others torn in half. There was no grass, and the bushes and small plants that grew near the thick trunks bore traces of where there had once been fruit. Perhaps they were bilberries: those who knew what they were like recalled their taste sadly.

Rebel, who was studying the patches of moss on the trunks that they were oh-so-slowly leaving behind, was worried he could not see much to eat. They were all hungry, and although their wish to find the new Dandelion Land gave them the strength to go on, the constantly falling leaves were a sign that they had to find a safe, warm and dark place where new life could begin.

The snails knew that life gave other creatures of the meadow clear, easily recognizable differences. Among spiders, for example, the male was small and the female was bigger. In their case, life had decided that it would be inside their shells that they had the two different parts that, by coming together, would create a third one.

A very short while before the frost and snow arrived, the snails could feel life's irresistible call for it to continue. So then, after an oh-so-slow ritual of rubbing their tentacles together, they prepared their bodies for the future of their kind. First one snail placed the tiny drops to be fertilized in another one's body. Then the other did the same. After that, they dug a deep hole, and in it they put the eggs of the future snails, protected by the dark dampness and safe from any predator.

Rebel knew this moment was approaching. They urgently needed to find a safe shelter and food.

Slowly, oh-so-slowly, the trees and patches of moss went by. The snails' progress became slower and harder. The clearing that the owl had told them about still seemed far away. They carried on until darkness fell over the wood. It was a darkness the snails had never known: however far they stretched their tentacles, they couldn't see any light from the stars.

"There's no moss on the trees any more," whispered Rebel. "Let's rest here until the light returns."

"What's the point? We'll never find the new Dandelion Land," one snail complained.

"How stupid to trust an old owl. You've been tricked," another one accused Rebel.

"We'll be safe under the leaves," whispered Rebel, but only a few of his friends followed his advice. Overwhelmed with tiredness and hunger, the others simply sank down in their shells.

When the pale light of dawn filtered into the wood, Rebel and his friends emerged from the covering of leaves they had slept under. What they saw made them very sad: all that was left of the snails who had not buried themselves were empty shells. They didn't know the wood, the creatures that lived there, or its dangers. They had to find the clearing to survive.

Slowly, oh-so-slowly, and still led by Rebel, the remaining snails continued their march. Some

of them felt so hungry that instead of going on they preferred to curl up in their shells and sleep a dreamless, hopeless sleep.

"The Dandelion Land is waiting for us. We will reach the Dandelion Land," whispered Rebel. These words gave him the strength to carry on.

ELEVEN

By the time they reached the clearing in the wood, they found that the cold had got there first. A blanket of frost covered the grass.

Rebel could not remember how many nights they had slept under the leaves in the wood. All he was sure of was that the number of snails was less than half those who had left their home beneath the calycanthus. Only the youngest had followed him to the end of the journey. Now with their tentacles they were staring at the new meadow covered in frost.

Lying in the middle of the meadow was a huge trunk, perhaps from a tree uprooted by an angry storm. Slowly, oh-so-slowly, they headed towards it. As they crawled on, Rebel turned his head to see if his friends were still following him. The trails of slime they were leaving behind looked to him like the marks of their pain.

The trunk seemed to them like a wonderful shelter. It was easy for them to crawl under, and they found not only the shade and warmth they needed for a home, but some grass that had not been crushed and scorched by the frost. The grass was not very delicious, but it did stop their hunger. They ate slowly – oh-so-slowly – until they were full.

CHAPTER ELEVEN

They prepared to spend their first night in this new home. They had no idea if they would be staying there, or if they were simply resting before carrying on. Before pulling his body inside his shell, Rebel glanced again at the trails of slime glistening on the frost. This time he thought that even though they were a mark of pain, they were also a sign of hope. He called to his friends to look at the trails so they would never forget them.

The measureless time of the slow meadow creatures went by, with more frost, snow and cold. The snails fell asleep for the winter. Their bodies only used enough energy for them to breathe slowly, oh-so-slowly, for their hearts to go on beating slowly, oh-so-slowly, and for them to grow slowly, oh-so-slowly.

At the end of this time without measure, they emerged from their sleep. When they raised their bodies out of their shells, the first thing they saw was Rebel. The eyes on the tips of his tentacles were staring at the meadow. The grass was grow-ing invitingly, the petals of the first wild flowers were opening: there was more than enough for them to eat. But Rebel was gazing at the place where their trails of slime had been.

"Look," he whispered.

All over what had been their trails, and as far as the first trees in the wood, grew delicious dandelion leaves.

"You did as you promised. You've brought us to Dandelion Land," said one snail joyfully.

"No," Rebel began to whisper. "I didn't bring you. But in this journey that I started when I wanted to know my name I've learnt many things. I learnt the importance of being slow. And now I have learnt that if we really want to reach it, Dandelion Land is inside us."

With that, Rebel crawled slowly, oh-so-slowly, over to eat with his friends.

Gothenburg, Winter 2012 –
Gijón, Summer 2013

Born in Santiago, Chile, Luis Sepúlveda is the multi-award-winning author of many adult novels and stories for children. Politically and socially engaged, he was persecuted and jailed by the Pinochet regime and worked for years as a crew member on a Greenpeace ship. His *Story of a Seagull and the Cat Who Taught Her to Fly* has been translated in over forty countries with several film and theatre adaptations.

IF YOU LIKED THIS STORY, WHY DON'T YOU TRY
LUIS SEPÚLVEDA'S MOVING STORY OF
A SEAGULL AND THE CAT WHO TAUGHT HER TO FLY?

Translated by Margaret Sayers Peden

A CAT, A SEAGULL, AN IMPOSSIBLE TASK

Caught up in an oil spill, a dying seagull scrambles ashore
to lay her final egg and lands on a balcony, where she meets
Zorba, a big black cat from the port of Hamburg. The cat
promises the seagull to look after the egg, not to eat the
chick once it's hatched and – most difficult of all – to teach
the baby gull to fly. Will Zorba and his feline friends hon-
our the promise and give Lucky, the adopted little seagull,
the strength to discover her true nature?

Luis Sepúlveda's instant classic is presented here with new
drawings by acclaimed illustrator Satoshi Kitamura.

5 MILLION COPIES SOLD WORLDWIDE!

Now turn the page and read a short extract from
The Story of a Seagull and the Cat Who Taught Her to Fly

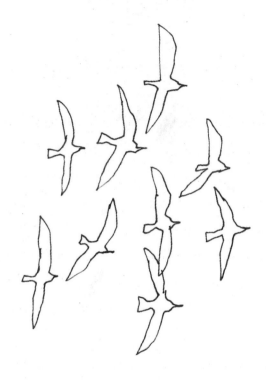

ONE

The North Sea

"School of herring port side!" the lookout gull announced, and the flock from the Red Sand Lighthouse received the news with shrieks of relief.

They had been flying for six hours without a break, and although the pilot gulls had found currents of warm air that made for pleasant gliding above the waves, they needed to renew their strength — and what better for that than a good mess of herring?

They were flying over the mouth of the Elbe River, where it flows into the North Sea. From high above they saw ships lining up one after the other like patient and disciplined whales waiting their turn to swim out to open sea. Once there, the flock would get their bearings and spread out towards all the ports of the planet.

Kengah, a female gull with feathers the colour of silver, especially liked to observe the ships' flags, for she knew that every one of them represented a way of speaking, of naming the same things with different words.

"Humans really have hard work of it," Kengah had once commented to a fellow she-gull. "Not at all like us gulls, who screech the same the world round."

"You're right. And most amazing of all is that sometimes they manage to understand one another," her gull friend had squawked.

Beyond the shoreline, the landscape turned bright green. Kengah could see an enormous pasture dotted with flocks of sheep grazing under the protection of the dykes and the lazy vanes of the windmills.

Following instructions from the pilot gulls, the flock from Red Sand Lighthouse seized a current of cold air and dived towards the shoal of herrings. One hundred and twenty bodies sliced into the water like arrows, and when they came to the surface each gull had a herring in its bill.

Tasty herring. Tasty and fat. Precisely what they needed to renew their energy before continuing their flight towards Den Helder, where they were to join the flock from the Frisian Islands.

According to their flight plan, they would then fly on to Calais, in the strait of Dover, and on through the English Channel, where they would be met by flocks from the Bay of the Seine and the Gulf of Saint-Malo. Then they would fly together till they reached the skies over the Bay of Biscay.

By then there would be a thousand gulls, a swiftly moving silver cloud that would be enlarged by the addition of flocks from Belle-Île-en-Mer, the Île d'Oléron, Cape Machichaco, Cape Ajo, and Cape Peñas. When all the gulls authorized by the law of the sea and the winds gathered over the Bay of Biscay, the Grand Convention of the Baltic and North Seas and the Atlantic Ocean could begin.

It would be a beautiful time, Kengah thought as she gulped down her third herring. As they did every year, they would listen to interesting stories, especially the ones told by the gulls from Cape Peñas, tireless voyagers who sometimes flew as far as the Canaries or Cape Verde Islands.

Female gulls like her would devote themselves to feasting on sardines and squid, while the males prepared nests at the edge of a cliff. There the female gulls would lay their eggs and hatch them, safe from any threat, and then, after the chicks lost their down and grew their first real feathers, would come the most beautiful part of the journey: teaching the fledglings to fly in the Bay of Biscay.

Kengah ducked her head to catch her fourth herring, and as a result she didn't hear the squawk of alarm that shattered the air: "Danger to port! Emergency take-off!"

When Kengah lifted her head from the water, she found herself all alone in the immensity of the ocean.

OTHER ILLUSTRATED TITLES
PUBLISHED IN OUR ALMA JUNIOR LIST

GREAT STORIES BEAUTIFULLY ILLUSTRATED

———————

Gabriel-Ernest and Other Tales, by Saki
illustrated by Quentin Blake

The Little Prince, by Antoine de Saint-Exupéry
illustrated by the Author

Dracula, by Bram Stoker
illustrated by David Mackintosh

The Hound of the Baskervilles, by Arthur Conan Doyle
illustrated by David Mackintosh

The Selfish Giant and Other Stories, by Oscar Wilde
illustrated by Philip Waechter

The New Teacher, by Dominique Demers
illustrated by Tony Ross

The Mysterious Librarian, by Dominique Demers
illustrated by Tony Ross

The Complete Peter Pan, by J.M. Barrie
illustrated by Joel Stewart

Arsène Lupin vs Sherlock Holmes, by Maurice Leblanc
illustrated by Thomas Müller

Robinson Crusoe, by Daniel Defoe
illustrated by Adam Stower

Treasure Island, by Robert Louis Stevenson
illustrated by David Mackintosh

The Castle of Inside Out, by David Henry Wilson
illustrated by Chris Riddell

Belle and Sébastien, by Cécile Aubry
illustrated by Helen Stephens

The Bears' Famous Invasion of Sicily, by Dino Buzzati
illustrated by the Author

The Wizard of Oz, by L. Frank Baum
illustrated by Ella Okstad

Lassie Come-Home, by Eric Knight
illustrated by Gary Blythe

The Adventures of Pipì the Pink Monkey, by Collodi
illustrated by Axel Scheffler

Just So Stories, by Rudyard Kipling
illustrated by the Author

The Jungle Books, by Rudyard Kipling
illustrated by Ian Beck

Five Children and It, by E. Nesbit
illustrated by Ella Okstad

How to Get Rid of a Vampire, J.M. Erre
illustrated by Clémence Lallemand

Anne of Green Gables, by L.M. Montgomery
illustrated by Susan Hellard

Pollyanna, by Eleanor H. Porter
illustrated by Kate Hindley

Little Women, by Louisa May Alcott
illustrated by Ella Bailey

Black Beauty, by Anna Sewell
illustrated by Paul Howard

Alistair Grim's Odditorium, by Gregory Funaro
illustrated by Chris Mould

Alistair Grim's Odd Aquaticum, by Gregory Funaro
illustrated by Adam Stower

The Secret Garden, by Frances Hodgson Burnett
illustrated by Peter Bailey

Alice's Adventures in Wonderland, by Lewis Carroll
illustrated by John Tenniel

Little Lord Fauntleroy, by Frances Hodgson Burnett
illustrated by Peter Bailey

The Railway Children, by E. Nesbit
illustrated by Peter Bailey

The Wind in the Willows, by Kenneth Grahame
illustrated by Tor Freeman

What Katy Did, by Susan Coolidge
illustrated by Susan Hellard

The Adventures of Sherlock Holmes, by Arthur Conan Doyle
illustrated by David Mackintosh

For our complete list, please visit:
www.almajunior.com